When I Feel Angry

WRITTEN BY Cornelia Maude Spelman
ILLUSTRATED BY Nancy Cote

Your AV² Media Enhanced book gives you a fiction readalong online. Log on to www.av2books.com and enter the unique book code from this page to use your readalong.

AV² Readalong Navigation

Go to **www.av2books.com**, and enter this book's unique code.

BOOK CODE

L951546

AV² by Weigl brings you media enhanced books that support active learning.

First Published by

ALBERT WHITMAN & COMPANY
Publishing children's books since 1919

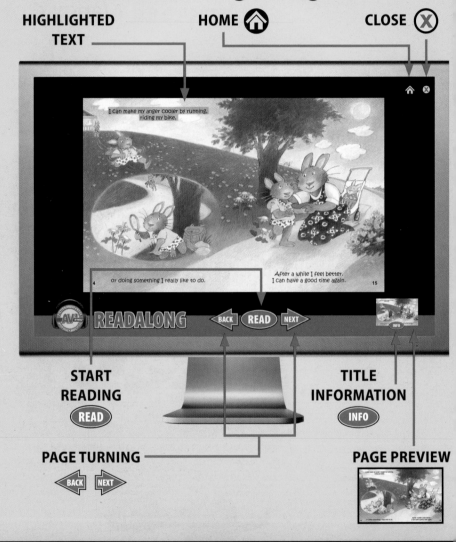

HIGHLIGHTED TEXT

HOME 🏠

CLOSE ⊗

START READING
READ

TITLE INFORMATION
INFO

PAGE TURNING
BACK NEXT

PAGE PREVIEW

Published by AV² by Weigl
350 5th Avenue, 59th Floor New York, NY 10118
Copyright ©2013 AV² by Weigl

052012
WEP160512

Library of Congress Cataloging-in-Publication Data

Spelman, Cornelia.
 When I feel angry / written by Cornelia Maude Spelman ; illustrated by Nancy Cote.
   p. cm.
 Summary: A little rabbit describes what makes her angry and the different ways she can control her anger.
 ISBN 978-1-61913-139-2 (hardcover : alk. paper)
 [1. Anger--Fiction. 2. Rabbits--Fiction.] I. Cote, Nancy, ill. II. Title.
 PZ7.S74727Wh 2012
 [E]--dc23
                                2012021690

Text copyright © 2000 by Cornelia Maude Spelman.
Illustrations copyright © 2000 by Nancy Cote.
Published in 2000 by Albert Whitman & Company.

* Note to Parents *

Everybody feels angry sometimes. While we can't avoid the feeling of anger, we can prevent acting in angry ways that hurt others. The distinction between feeling an emotion and acting upon it is important. Helping our children make this distinction and helping them manage their anger without hurting others are among our most important tasks.

We need to teach our children ways to manage uncomfortable and unpleasant feelings. Some ways to manage anger are outlined in this book; you and your children may find others that work for you. Praise and encouragement when your children are successful at recognizing and managing their emotions will reinforce their comfort and feelings of competence.

No matter what we say, children learn most by our example. So we must know how to manage our own angry feelings. Many of us were not helped to do this. Perhaps we learned that expressing our feelings, even our most negative ones, was all that was necessary. Now it's known, however, that simply expressing anger without knowing how to reduce and resolve it can lead to its escalation and to violence in words and deeds.

When we adults fail to control our own anger and speak or act in hurtful ways, we should apologize and set a better example the next time. In this way we show that we mean what we say. We demonstrate that we value resolving conflicts in ways that do not hurt others, and we and our children increase the possibility of a more peaceful world.

— Cornelia Maude Spelman, A.C.S.W., L.C.S.W.

When somebody makes fun of me,

I feel angry.

5

I feel angry when I have to stop a game
at the best part and clean up my room,

or, when we finally can go swimming, it rains.

It makes me mad when I try my hardest but I can't make my drawing look right. I just crumple it up and throw it away.

If the teacher says I was talking and I wasn't, I get angry. It isn't fair!

Anger is a strong, hot feeling.

When I feel angry, I want to say
something mean, or yell, or hit.

But feeling like I want to is not the same
as doing it. Feeling can't hurt anyone
or get me in trouble, but doing can.

When I want to say something mean, or yell,
or hit, there are other things I can do.

I can go away from the person I'm angry with.
I can take deep breaths and blow the air out,
hard, to send the anger out of me.

I can make my anger cooler by running,
riding my bike,

14   or doing something I really like to do.

After a while I feel better.
I can have a good time again.

Some things that make me angry can't
be changed, like when our team loses,

or my favorite thing gets spoiled.

But sometimes when I feel angry, it means something needs to be different. Maybe it's me. Maybe I need to rest or cry.

Maybe I need time by myself.

Maybe someone else needs to be different.
Maybe someone needs to be nicer to me,
or to stop being unfair.

I might need help figuring it all out.

Then I can change what I'm doing.
Or I can tell someone else what I need.
I can listen to the other person tell, too.
Talking and listening usually make things better.

When I feel angry, I don't have to stay angry.
I can cool down so I don't hurt someone
or get into trouble.

I can go away.

I can take deep breaths and blow them out.
I can run, ride my bike, or play with my toys.
I can rest or cry.

I can figure out what made me angry,
or ask someone to help me.

I can talk, and I can listen.

When I feel angry,
I know what to do!